The Shortstop
Who Knew Too Much

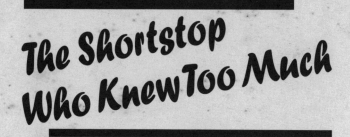

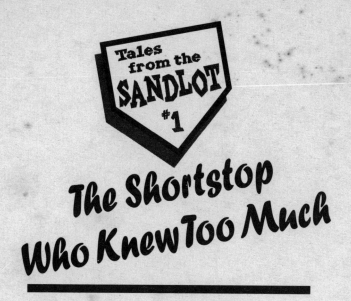

Tales from the SANDLOT #1

The Shortstop Who Knew Too Much

Dan Gutman

AN **APPLE** PAPERBACK

SCHOLASTIC INC.

New York Toronto London Auckland Sydney

No part of this publication may be reproduced in whole or in part, or stored in a retrieval system, or transmitted in any form or by any means, electronic, mechanical, photocopying, recording, or otherwise, without written permission of the publisher. For information regarding permission, write to Scholastic Inc., 555 Broadway, New York, NY 10012.

ISBN 0-590-13760-3

Text copyright © 1997 by Dan Gutman.
Illustrations copyright © 1997 by Scholastic Inc.
All rights reserved. Published by Scholastic Inc.
APPLE PAPERBACKS and the APPLE PAPERBACKS logo are trademarks and/or registered trademarks of Scholastic Inc.

12 11 10 9 8 7 6 5   8 9/9 0 1 2/0

Printed in the U.S.A.

First Scholastic printing, April 1997

To Liza Voges

Contents

Chapter 1

The Beaning

"Duck!!!"

For a millisecond or two, I thought about moving my head backward so the baseball would *whoosh* by in front of me. For another millisecond, I thought about moving my head forward so the ball would zip behind me.

Unfortunately, I ran out of milliseconds. I simply stood there, frozen, like a statue. "Duck!" was the last word I heard before the ball exploded against my head.

For a small object, a baseball packs a wallop. I felt like I'd been hit by a train.

My batting helmet probably saved my life. The ball smacked into it hard, just above the earflap.

There's a lot of cushioning in the helmet, but a good fastball still rattles your brain pretty good. If I wasn't wearing a helmet, I might not be telling you this story.

But I was, so I will.

Chapter 2

Jake and Whip

When the pitch hit me, I collapsed like a rag doll right there in the batter's box. Later, I was told that my parents were out of the stands and on the field before I hit the ground.

My mom apparently dashed out, screaming "Jake! Jake! My baby!" and cradled my head in her arms. It would have been really embarrassing had I been conscious. But I didn't even hear the siren of the ambulance when it pulled up. I was down for the count. Lights out.

The pitch came from the hand of William "Whiplash" Witherspoon, commonly known as the "The Whip" around here ("here" being Somerville, a small town in central New Jersey). Whip is a tall stringbean of a kid with a left arm that stretches

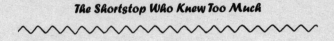

nearly down to his knees. It's like, well, it's like a whip.

Even though we play on different teams and Whip goes to private school, we're best friends. We grew up around the corner from each other. We're both only children, so Whip and I have been like brothers for as long as I can remember.

One day last year Whip and I went to one of those places where they have batting cages and a radar gun that clocks the speed of your pitches. I could barely throw the ball 50 miles per hour. But Whip was getting it up past 70 miles per hour just about every time.

That's nearly major league heat! Not bad for a twelve-year-old kid. And with his submarine delivery, he makes it even harder on a left-handed batter like me to pick up the ball in flight. You don't want to get in the way of Whip's fastball, like I did.

When Whip and I first tried out for Little League together, the coaches took one look at his arm and they were drooling all over themselves. It was like they were seeing the second coming of Randy Johnson. Maybe they were.

In any case, Whip got picked first, by the Hornan Hornets, who were sponsored by a hardware

4

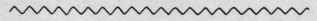

store in town. The Davidson One-Hour Martinizers, a dry cleaning store, took me as their third pick. I don't know what "martinizing" means, but they must know what they're doing because our uniforms are always nice and white and bright.

As I said before, Whip and I are like brothers. Well, brothers fight a lot. When Whip nearly took my head off with that fastball, it started a feud that just about ripped apart our friendship.

But that's not why I'm telling you this story. I'm telling you the story because when I came to after the beaning, I realized almost immediately that something was different about me.

Suddenly, I had the mysterious power of ESP.

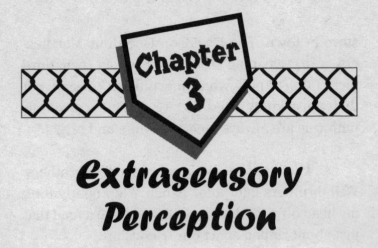

Extrasensory Perception

ESP. It's not the same as ESPN, the TV sports channel. ESP stands for "extrasensory perception." Mind reading. Supernatural stuff.

The bonk on the head did something to my brain. Suddenly, I was more aware of the world around me. My five senses felt stronger. Most astonishingly, I could look at someone and know exactly what they were *thinking*.

Don't get me wrong. I never believed in any of that psychic mumbo jumbo before. Every so often I'd see one of these nuts on TV pretending to read somebody's mind. Usually they guess what a member of the audience has in their pockets, or some

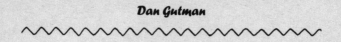

such stunt. They seem to be pretty good at it, but I figured it was all a trick.

As I was lying there in the dirt next to home plate, I realized that I had the power of ESP myself. And it was the real thing.

When I opened my eyes, a whole bunch of people were crowded around me. My folks, of course. My coach, Mr. Rosario. The coach of the Hornets. Kids on both teams. A few gawkers who I didn't even know — probably the same people who slow down their cars to stare at traffic accidents at the side of the road.

At first, I couldn't hear any of them speaking. Their mouths were moving and they were making lots of hand motions, but no speech was coming out. Instead, I could hear a bunch of other voices in my head — the voices of what they were *thinking*. It was like watching a foreign movie without the subtitles.

After a minute or so, my hearing returned. I could hear what people were saying *and* what they were thinking. It was pretty confusing at first.

My mom, of course, was hysterical. She was

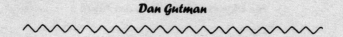

blubbering all over the place and shouting, "Give him air! Get a doctor over here!"

But I could also hear her thinking, **"I never should have let him try out for Little League. If he's hurt, I'll never forgive myself. It's all my fault,"** and stuff like that.

My dad seemed calmer on the outside. But when I focused my attention on him, I could tell he was thinking, **"Somebody's gonna pay for this. Who can I punch? Who can I sue? If Jake is hurt badly, they'll never play ball in this town again!"**

Coach Rosario wasn't saying anything out loud. He just had a worried look on his face. I could tell he was thinking, **"That's it. I'm in trouble now. Kids this age don't know how to get out of the way of a pitch. They shouldn't let Whip Witherspoon pitch in this league. He's too fast and too wild. I hope Jake's gonna be all right."**

It was pretty cool having all these grown-ups fuss over me while I read their minds.

A few of my teammates were huddled over me. They were also hoping I was going to be okay,

but I could tell that the biggest concern for some of them was, **"Does this mean we won't be going to Dairy Queen after the game?"**

The coach of the Hornets wasn't sympathetic at all. He leaned over me looking very concerned, but I knew it was an act. What he was thinking was, **"Oh man, this is just a warm-up game! If Whip's gonna knock somebody out, why can't he do it in a game that counts?"**

Some of the Hornets' parents had even nastier thoughts. One of them, I could tell, thought I was faking an injury. Another was happy it was a Martinizer who had been hit. One dad was glad that the best hitter on the Martinizers (that's me) might be out for a few games.

Man, Little League parents can be brutal.

At least they cared enough to gather around me. Whip, who was supposed to be my best friend, was nowhere in sight. It was impossible to know what he was thinking.

The crowd of people around me made an opening for a doctor, who had bounded out of the bleachers. "Don't move him!" he was shouting. "Don't move his head!"

He crouched down next to me and held my head in one position. I could read his mind effortlessly.

"Son, I'm Dr. Kielbasa, a neurologist affiliated with Saint Barnabas Hospital. My son plays on the Hornets."

"I'm Jake Miller," I said. "Dr. Kielbasa . . . like a sausage?"

"Yes, like a sausage."

I never heard of anybody named after a sausage, but who was I to argue? He seemed to know what he was doing.

"Looks like you've got a nice bump there, Jake," Dr. Kielbasa said.

"I'll be okay," I told him. "Two."

"Two?" he asked, puzzled. "Two *what*?"

"Weren't you going to ask me how many fingers you were holding up?"

"Well, yes, I was," he replied.

"And weren't you going to hold up two fingers?"

"Yes," he admitted. "I was."

"Well, there's your answer," I told him. "Two."

"Hmmmm," the doctor said, looking at me curiously. "Jake, I'm going to ask you a few simple

11

questions to make sure you haven't had a concussion. How do you spell cat?"

"C-A-T," I replied.

"Who was the sixteenth president?"

"Abraham Lincoln."

"What's two times two?"

"Four."

"What's four times four?"

"Sixteen."

"What's sixteen times sixteen?"

"Uh, we didn't get that far in the multiplication tables yet."

"What's the capital of Wisconsin?"

"I have no idea. Milwaukee, maybe?"

"You're going to be fine, Jake," the doctor said, "but I want to shoot some X rays, just to be on the safe side."

Slowly, the emergency medical crew lifted me onto a stretcher and hoisted it into the ambulance. I was finished with baseball for the day.

What a way to start the season!

Nice-Looking Brain

The ride to the hospital was pretty cool. I asked them to turn on the siren, but they told me they're only allowed to do that in emergencies. My folks followed the ambulance in their car and helped wheel me up to the radiology department for an X ray. When that was finished, we were instructed to go to Dr. Kielbasa's office.

"I feel fine now, Doc," I told him. "I don't have to miss any games, do I? My team needs me."

"I want you to sit out two weeks, Jake," he said. "That swelling needs to go down."

"Oh, man!"

"Jake, the doctor knows what he's talking about," said my dad.

Just then a technician came in with some X rays and handed them to the doctor. He clipped them to a box on the wall, flipped a switch to light them up, and peered at them.

"Frontal lobe looks fine. Cerebellum looks good. Did anyone ever tell you that you have a very nice medulla oblongata? Hmmmm . . ."

Mom quickly chimed in. "What do you mean — hmmmm? What do you see, doctor? What is it?"

I focused my attention on him and picked up his thoughts. **"Whoa! What's this? It's not exactly an injury, but I've never seen anything like it before. The boy seems fine, but something unusual is definitely going on in the cortex."**

"Doc," my dad said. "What is it?"

"Oh, nothing," he replied. "I was just admiring Jake's cerebral cortex. It looks like it's in tip-top shape."

"Is there anything else besides baseball he shouldn't do?" Mom asked.

"Yes," the doctor said, patting my back, "No homework for a year. Can you manage that, Jake?"

"Sure!"

"Just kidding," he said. "Keep him away from strenuous activity for two weeks, and make an

14

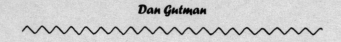

appointment with the receptionist to see me at that time."

As we left the office, I saw the doctor staring intently at the X rays with a puzzled look on his face.

Chapter 5

War with Whip

My folks brought me home from the hospital and put me to bed with a cold icepack to keep the swelling down. My head was throbbing, but I slept like a bear in December.

I woke up the next morning to the sound of a ringing telephone. Mom tiptoed into the room to see if I was awake. "It's Whip Witherspoon, honey," she whispered. "Can you talk?"

Whip and I have sort of a weird relationship. We're best friends, but we get into arguments a lot. One time we didn't talk for nearly a year. It was because I borrowed one of Whip's hockey sticks and accidentally broke it when I tried to use it as a can opener.

Anyway, this time I was furious with Whip. Just before the game, we'd had a silly argument. It

was over a girl. Whip said he liked Rosalie Minder, who was the queen of the Somerville Fall Festival parade this year. I said I liked her, too. Whip said I couldn't have her because she was his. I said he couldn't have her because she was mine. We were on the verge of duking it out.

Rosalie Minder, I'm sure, didn't even know either of us existed. I mean, guys in my class are always *talking* about girls, but none of us have ever actually been on a *date* or anything. I still feel a little creepy just talking with most girls.

Still, Whip and I got pretty steamed over Rosalie. I was convinced that he had beaned me on purpose. I picked up the phone with an attitude.

"Hey, man," Whip said, "I heard they X-rayed your brain and found nothing." Whip laughed nervously.

"What do *you* want?" I demanded in my meanest voice.

"I'm kidding, man, *kidding*!" Whip said. "Are you okay, Jake? I feel terrible, man. I'm sorry I hit you. The pitch got away from me. You believe me, don't you, Jake?"

"Are you finished?" I asked.

"Yeah," he said. "That's all I have to say, man."

"Apology not accepted, Whip."

"But . . ."

"You beaned me on purpose! You could have *killed* me! And you didn't even stick around to see if I was okay. That's what burns me up! And now you expect me to forgive you? Forget it, Whip."

"I ran away!" Whip said, flustered. "I was so upset that I didn't finish the game. I was afraid you were dead, man! I thought I had killed my best friend! I went home crying. If you don't believe me, ask my mom."

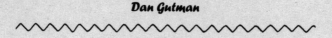

"That's a lot of baloney," I said. "I don't need to ask your mom and I don't want to speak with you again."

"What about the Mustang?" he asked softly. Whip and I were building a model car over at his house.

"Finish it yourself," I said. "I don't want to see your face."

I meant it, too.

Chapter 6

The Secret Weapon

Whip and I were through as buddies, but I made lots of new friends — thanks to my ESP.

At first I didn't tell anybody what I had discovered about myself. I wanted to see how powerful my new talent was, and what I could do with it.

Coach Rosario (who wasn't fired after all) had me suit up and watch our first few games from the bench.

"Use this opportunity to learn the fine points of the game," he instructed. "See if their pitcher is telegraphing his pitches. Try and steal some signs. You can't use your body, so get your head into the game."

It was pretty boring, but sitting on the bench gave me plenty of time to think. And thinking was

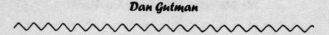

an activity which had become much more interesting for me since I learned I had ESP.

In my first game as a benchwarmer, we were playing the Pathmark Panthers, a pretty decent team that was sponsored by a local supermarket. In the first inning I was minding my own business, concentrating on the game, when a voice in my head said — as clear as a bell — **"Curveball, outside corner."**

Sure enough, on the next pitch, the Panther pitcher tossed a nice, slow curve that just nicked the plate. The umpire called it strike one. Somehow, I had read the mind of the pitcher!

I wanted to see if I could do it again. On the next pitch I directed all of my attention on the pitcher.

"Heater," he thought. **"Keep it low."**

And there it was, a fastball at the knees.

This was interesting! I could read the other team's signs.

As the game went on, I discovered that I was able to predict every pitch. When I concentrated

21

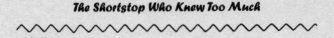

on the base runner, I could tell when he was going to attempt a steal. By concentrating on the coach, I knew in advance if he was going to call for a hit-and-run play. If he told his hitter to take a pitch or swing away, I knew it in advance.

It was was like reading tomorrow's newspaper today.

In the third inning we were ahead 6–4. When the Panthers got a guy on base, I sidled over to Molly Carver, our second baseman. She was sitting out the game because of a sprained ankle. She's the smartest kid in my class, and she knows it.

"Say, Molly," I whispered. "Wanna see me predict the next three times their runners try to steal?"

"Can't be done," she said, spitting a sunflower seed on the grass. "Impossible."

I focused all my attention on the runner at first. I didn't pick up any signals on the first two pitches, but just before the third pitch I heard the runner's voice in my head: **"This is it. I'm going!"**

"Watch the base runner," I said to Molly. "I bet he takes off on the next pitch."

"No way," said Molly. "That guy never runs."

But sure enough, as soon as our pitcher went into his windup, the runner broke from first. Our catcher, Bubba Bradley, caught the pitch cleanly, but the runner was safe at second by three steps.

Bubba is good at blocking the plate, but he's slow as a moose. The only way he ever throws anybody out is when we call a pitchout, and Coach Rosario doesn't like to do that much because a pitchout is an automatic ball (of course) and that leaves our pitcher behind in the count.

"Lucky guess, Jake," said Molly, spitting another sunflower seed on the grass.

"Maybe it was, and maybe it wasn't," I replied. "Care to make it interesting?"

"What do you mean?"

Molly is a card collector extraordinaire. She's got a Ken Griffey, Jr., rookie card that I've had my eye on just about since Griffey was a rookie.

"If I predict the next two steal attempts, you give me your Ken Griffey, Jr., rookie card."

She thought about that for a moment. Finally, she replied, "And what do I get if you miss?"

"If I'm wrong," I said seriously, "I'll give you my 1990 Barry Bonds."

"You've got a 1990 Bobby Bonilla, too, don't you?"

"Yeah, I do."

"Throw in Bonilla and you've got a deal."

Molly drives a hard bargain. But what did I have to worry about? I could read minds!

"You're on," I said.

Molly and I watched the game with renewed interest. The Panthers didn't get another runner on base until the next inning. A tall kid with long hair. He danced off the bag looking like he wanted to steal, but I didn't catch any thoughts of taking off. The pitch came in and their batter swung through it. Strike one.

"So when's he gonna steal, hotshot?" Molly asked me. She was furiously chewing and spitting out sunflower seeds.

As soon as the runner got back to first base, I picked up a thought: **"I'm taking second now. I hope my dad is watching."**

"Now!" I whispered to Molly.

Sure enough, the runner took off on the pitch and slid into second ahead of Bubba's late throw.

"Man, you are lucky!" Molly said, shaking her head.

"All skill," I gloated. "All skill."

"You still need to predict one more."

"No problemo, amigo."

The next batter singled, scoring the runner from second and making the score Martinizers 6, Panthers 5. I noticed a few beads of sweat gathering on Molly's forehead. She didn't want to lose that Griffey card.

"Getting a little nervous, Molly?" I asked. "Want to call off the bet?"

"No," she said curtly. "No way you're gonna predict three steal attempts in a row."

"Just watch me," I told her. "Watch and learn from the master."

I scoped out the runner at first. He was a bit overweight and didn't look like a big threat to steal. He took a very small lead. If this kid had any thoughts at all in his head, I couldn't pick them up.

Coach Rosario went out to the mound to have a little chat and settle down our pitcher, Joey Risko. While he was out there, I focused my attention on the other coach.

"What's that bozo doing on the mound?" he was thinking. "I don't have time for this. I gotta get home early tonight. I'm gonna send the runner on the first pitch. I don't care if he's out by a mile."

I leaned over to Molly. "First pitch," I whispered. "I say the runner goes on the first pitch, and your Griffey card is mine."

"You're nuts!" Molly retorted.

As Coach Rosario came off the mound, he sat on the bench between me and Molly. "What are you two gabbing about?" he asked. "Your heads are supposed to be in the game."

"Our heads are in the game, Coach," I told him. "We're discussing strategy."

"Yeah, Coach," Molly chimed in. "Jake claims the runner's gonna steal on the first pitch. I say he's out of his mind."

Coach Rosario surveyed the field. "I agree with Molly," he said. "First of all, the guy on first is the slowest runner on their team. Their best hitter is up, and there are two outs. If the guy is thrown out stealing, it takes the bat out of the hitter's hand. It doesn't make sense to try a steal in this situation."

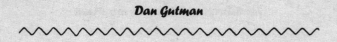
We all turned to the field. Our fielders took their positions. The runner took his lead. Joey went into his windup.

I could see Molly's and Coach Rosario's jaws drop open when the runner broke from first. Bubba got off a better-than-usual throw, but our second baseman dropped the peg and the runner barreled in safely in a cloud of dust.

"Griffey is mine!" I shouted triumphantly.

"Shoot!" Molly said disgustedly, spraying a mouthful of sunflower shells across the bench.

Coach Rosario eyed me suspiciously. "How did you know that guy was going to steal?" he asked.

"Just a hunch, Coach," I said, beaming.

"He just predicted their last three steals, Coach," revealed Molly. "He must have stolen their signs."

"Do you have their signs, Jake?"

"It's more like a sixth sense, Coach," I said, honestly.

Coach Rosario turned back toward the field. The Panthers had a runner at second now. The score was 6–5 in our favor and it was the sixth inning.

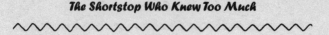

"Okay," Coach said to me. "Lemme see your sixth sense in action."

"Gee, I don't want to show off, Coach."

"Sounds like you don't want to win the ballgame, either," he replied.

He had a point. If I truly could read minds, I owed it to the team to use this power and help us win games, not just win baseball cards for myself.

I turned my attention to the Panthers' coach. Joey had just thrown ball four and the Panther hitter trotted to first base. That made it runners on first and second, nobody out, in the sixth inning. The Panthers needed a run to tie, and two to win the game. The girl at the plate usually got her bat on the ball.

Their coach was scratching his chin, and I picked up what he was thinking: **"If I send both runners, that will force the infielders to cover second and third base. It opens up huge holes to hit a ball through. If I give my hitter the sign to hit away, she just might poke a grounder through one of those holes. We score one run for sure, and maybe two."** He started flashing signs.

"Coach," I said, tapping him on the shoulder.

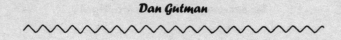

"They're hitting and running. Both runners are gonna go with the pitch, and the batter is gonna swing away."

"Get outta here!" he scoffed.

"Well, you asked."

Coach Rosario looked me in the eye. "This is insane," he said. "But I think you know something I don't know."

With that, he got up and walked out to the mound. The infielders gathered around him, and after a minute or so Coach returned to the bench.

"I told Joey and Bubba to do a pitchout," he told me. "If you're wrong, I'm gonna look like a real monkey."

The runners took their leads from first and second. The hitter squeezed her bat tightly. As Joey went into his windup, Bubba slid out from behind the plate for a surprise pitchout.

The batter, who had been ordered to swing no matter what, flailed wildly, flinging her bat at the ball and striking out. One out.

The runners, who had been ordered to go with the pitch, couldn't turn back. Bubba pumped the ball to third to nail one of them. Two outs.

The runner on second got confused when he

saw that we had called for a pitchout. He stopped in his tracks between second and third. We got him in a rundown and he was dead meat. Three outs.

Triple play! Game over. We win. Incredible!

Coach Rosario looked at me with this wild look in his eyes. "What do you know that I don't know?" he asked.

"Lots," I replied mysteriously.

After the game, when everybody was shaking hands, the Panther coach came over to Coach Rosario at our bench.

"What made you decide to pitch out?" the Panther coach asked Coach Rosario. "That wrecked my whole strategy."

"A little birdie told me to," laughed Coach Rosario, winking at me.

Chapter 7

The System

Coach Rosario realized — even better than I did — that my little mental gift had the potential to win lots of games for us. He installed me as the third base coach with strict instructions: "Steal every sign you can steal. Let me know whatever you find out."

We worked out a complicated sign system. If I knew a fastball was coming, I would swipe one hand across the letters of my uniform. For a curveball, I'd swipe my hand twice. If I suspected a steal, I would touch my nose with my right thumb. For the hit-and-run, I'd take off my cap and put it back on. If the hitter was swinging away, I'd clap my hands together three times and shout, "Hmmm baby!" I also threw in a bunch of meaningless signs to throw off our opponents.

Naturally, we would rotate these signs, some-times between innings. The last thing we wanted was to steal somebody's signs and then have them steal their signs *back*.

Thanks to my ESP, the Martinizers were un-beatable. I would stand in the third base box and watch everything. Every time the catcher called for a curve, I knew it and flashed the sign to our hitter. When their pitcher cranked up the fast one, we were ready for it.

Bubba Bradley was throwing out base stealers like he was Ivan Rodriguez. That's because every time the other team was going to steal, I relayed the information to Coach Rosario and he'd call for a pitchout. It got so that other teams simply stopped trying to steal bases on Bubba.

My powers were uncanny. Opposing coaches would leave the field shaking their heads in amaze-ment and frustration. They knew something was going on with me, but they didn't know what it was.

Chapter 8

Back in the Game

"Can I play ball again, Doc? Can I?"

Two weeks after the beaning I went back to Dr. Kielbasa for a checkup. He felt my head all over and seemed satisfied that the swelling had gone down.

"How do you feel?" he asked.

"Great!" I exclaimed. "All better."

"Any side effects?"

"Nothing special."

"What do you mean, nothing special?"

I wasn't going to tell him about the ESP. But then I figured he *is* my doctor, and it might be important for him to know.

"Ever since the beaning I've been finding that I can sort of read people's thoughts," I explained

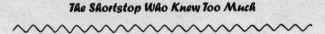

sheepishly. "I know it sounds crazy, but I hear their voices in my head."

"Hmmmm," he said, stroking his chin. "A knock on the head has been known to effect brain functioning, but usually in a *negative* way. Is there any possibility that you're just imagining these voices?"

"It's possible, Doctor, but it seems awfully real."

"Hmmmm. Jake, I'd like to shoot an MRI to get a better look at your brain."

"What's an MRI?" I asked.

"It stands for magnetic resonance imaging. It's basically a picture of the inside of the body that is much clearer than an X ray. It doesn't hurt or anything. We only have one machine at the hospital, and it'll be a couple of weeks until I can schedule an appointment for you, but I think we should check this out."

"Can I play ball until then?"

"Sure, Jake," Dr. Kielbasa said. "Just try not to get hit in the head again, okay?"

The next day I asked Coach Rosario to put me in the game.

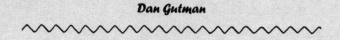

"I don't know, Jake . . ." he said.

A quick read of his mind told me he was afraid my parents might sue him if I got hit by another pitch or injured in some way.

"Don't worry," I assured him. "My folks aren't going to sue you. The beaning was my fault. I didn't react quickly enough. I should have bailed out of the batter's box. It won't happen again, Coach. I promise. The doctor said it was okay for me to play."

"All right," he agreed reluctantly, penciling me in my old number three position on his lineup card.

Comeback Player of the Year

As soon as I was allowed to swing a bat again, I began tearing the cover off the ball. I had always been a decent hitter, but when I knew what pitches were coming I was like Babe Ruth, Ty Cobb, and Ted Williams all rolled into one. The ball looked like a melon to me. Soon the Martinizers were way ahead of the rest of the National League.

One day after school, the mail came and my mom handed me a letter . . .

Dear Jake, man,

I know you're still mad. Nothing I can do about that. I can't take the pitch back, much as I

wish I could. But you gotta believe me, man. It wasn't on purpose! That argument we had before the game was stupid. It had nothing to do with it. The pitch just got away. Please believe me.

Well, I'm glad to see the Martinizers are doing so well. From what I hear, you're hitting like Frank Thomas. The Hornets are doing pretty well, too. Maybe we'll meet in the World Series.

Your friend?

William "Whiplash" Witherspoon

If I had seen the words "I'm sorry" in there, I might have been moved. I crumpled Whip's letter up and threw it in the garbage.

I had been following the progress of the Hornets myself. Whip was having an incredible year, leading the American League in strikeouts and earned run average. He hardly ever walked anyone, and he hadn't hit a single batter since the day he brained me in the warm-up game.

If the Martinizers won the pennant in the National League and the Hornets won the American League pennant, there would be a one-game World Series to determine the Somerville Little League Champion. The winning team would not only get

bragging rights as the best Little League team in town, but the mayor of Somerville announced they would also win a free trip to the Baseball Hall of Fame in Cooperstown, New York, over summer vacation.

Cooperstown! Disneyland for baseball fans. Just the word made my mouth water.

If It Ain't Broke, Don't Fix It

It didn't take long before everybody on the Martinizers knew I had this "special gift" to read minds. Coach Rosario had anticipated problems, and he gathered us around him at home plate before practice one day.

"Kids," he announced, "as many of you know, ever since Jake was hit on the noggin in the warm-up game, he's had this ... uh ... talent. He can't explain it and neither can I. But you can see how it's helping us win ball games. It's like having an extra bat in our lineup. Two bats, really.

"But, kids, I think it would be best for the team if we keep this secret weapon secret, at least until the season is over. No point in telling the rest of

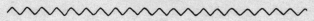

the teams just yet. We're in position to win the championship this year and make it all the way to Cooperstown. I don't want anything to mess up our chances.

"So raise your hands, if you're with me, and let's all swear on the plate here that Jake's talent will be our little secret. Okay? Great! Now let's take some batting practice."

I noticed that Molly was the only Martinizer who didn't raise her hand.

I was doing my stretching exercises before the game the next day when I noticed Molly scowling at me. I figured she was still sore about the Griffey card, and that I should try and patch things up with her.

"How's it going, Molly?" I said, strolling over to her.

"Why bother asking?" she replied angrily. "Just read my mind and you'll *know* how it's going!"

With that crack, she walked away in a huff. I caught up with her and put a hand on her shoulder. "Hey, are you still upset about that Griffey card?"

"No," she said. "I'm upset because you tricked

41

me! You've got ESP. You know everything that's gonna happen! That's not fair! It's cheating! Why don't you try using your own skill for a change?"

She ripped her shoulder away from my hand and walked away again.

"I'll give you the card back!" I shouted after her. "I didn't mean to cheat you!"

"Keep the stupid card!" she said firmly, turning to face me. "When I make an agreement with somebody, I stick with it. Get some scruples, Jake!"

Scruples? I didn't even know what scruples were, much less where I could get some. And all the stores were closed by that time anyhow. But I looked the word up as soon as I got home.

Scruples: A moral or ethical consideration that acts as a restraining force or inhibits certain actions.

Huh? I was still a little fuzzy on what scruples were, but maybe Molly had a point. It wasn't exactly fair for one team to have a player with ESP while none of the other teams do. We were winning games on false pretenses.

On the other hand, I thought, a player should use every tool he has to help his team. There's

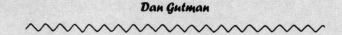

nothing in the rule book that says you're not allowed to read the minds of your opponents.

Even if there *was* a rule against mind reading, bending the rules of baseball is one of the game's long-standing traditions. After all, Gaylord Perry admitted he threw spitballs his entire career, and he's a member of the Baseball Hall of Fame today.

I didn't feel all that good about using my mind-reading powers, but decided to stick with them. We were winning, and I was having too much fun to stop.

As long as I was going to use my power, I figured, I might as well use it to the max.

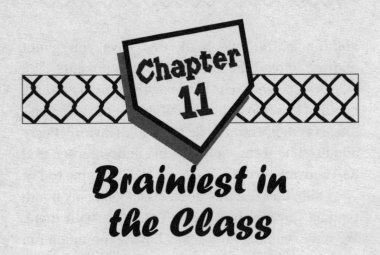

Chapter 11

Brainiest in the Class

I was always a fairly average student in school. I was never the teacher's pet, and I didn't sit in "the dumb row" either. But it's amazing how easy school becomes when you have ESP. Knowing what the teacher is thinking makes you look a lot smarter. My grades shot up, and soon I was challenging Molly Carver for "brainiest" in the class.

We were doing geography one day and Mrs. Cameron-Sears was grilling us on state capitals.

"Okay, everybody, who can tell me the capital of Washington?"

Molly's hand went up. I focused my attention on the teacher. She was thinking, **"Ha-ha. I'll bet they think it's Seattle. Well, I'll fool**

them. It's really Olympia."

"Molly?"

"The capital of Washington is Seattle," Molly said.

"No. Good guess, though. Anyone else?"

I raised my hand.

"Jake?"

"The capital of Washington is Olympia," I announced.

"Very *good*, Jake! How about Wisconsin? Who can tell me the capital?"

Molly and I raised our hands. Mrs. Cameron-Sears gestured toward me. I knew she was trying to trip us up and say Milwaukee.

"Madison!" I proclaimed.

"Very *good*," she said, obviously impressed. "You must have been studying your state capitals, Jake."

"I have, Mrs. Cameron-Sears," I lied. I looked at Molly out the corner of my eye, and she had the meanest face I had ever seen.

Except for Molly, the other players on the Martinizers had become my best friends. They knew I was leading them to the trip to Cooperstown. Besides, they probably figured that if I could read their minds whenever I wanted to, they'd better be thinking good thoughts about me.

I was at my locker before lunch one day when Ramon Martinez, our first baseman, came over to me.

"Jake," he said. "Will you do me a big favor?"

"Sure, Ramon, what is it?"

"There's this girl I kinda like."

"Uh-huh."

"Shari Samuels."

46

"Yeah," I said. "I know who she is. She's cute."

"I want to ask her out."

"So go ahead, Ramon," I replied. "Ask her out."

He looked at me and paused. "I think you know what's holding me back," Ramon said reluctantly.

I looked at Ramon and focused in. Oh! He doesn't want to ask Shari out because he's afraid she doesn't like him. He doesn't want to be turned down and made into a fool. He wants *me* to find out if Shari likes him *before* he takes a chance and asks her out.

Ingenious, I must say.

"Sure, Ramon," I said, throwing an arm around his shoulder. "Let's give it a shot."

Ramon and I strolled into the cafeteria, got our food, and scoped out the place. Ramon spotted Shari sitting with three other girls and gestured with his head where she was. We found two seats nearby.

"Tune in, Jake," said Ramon, tearing the paper off his straw.

I focused in on the table where Shari was sitting. The girls were jabbering about a science test Mrs. Hamilton was giving next week. But when I

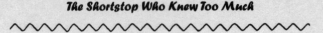

read their minds, I was amazed to find that none of them was actually thinking about the test.

"You getting anything, Jake?" whispered Ramon, jabbing me with an elbow.

"Yeah," I said. "Lots. This is fascinating."

"Fill me in, man!"

This is what each girl was thinking . . .

Alexandra Dimetropolis: **"If I could lose just five pounds, I'd be perfect. Perfect! What am I, crazy? People don't judge you by how much you weigh! Well, they shouldn't, but they still do. Why should I care what people think, anyway? I'm so confused!"**

Barbara Trotta: **"If I run for class president, I will rule the school! But if I lose, I'll be the laughingstock. Boy, Alexandra looks skinny today. If I looked like that, I wouldn't even bother running for president. I'd be popular already."**

Diane Meier: **"I wish Barbara would shut up. She's so boring! Why is it that the dullest people talk the most about themselves? My life is infinitely more interesting than hers and I haven't said anything yet."**

~~~~~~~~~~~~~~~~~~~~~~~~~~~~~~

Shari Samuels: **"Brad Pitt . . ."**

"Sorry old boy," I informed Ramon, "you're barking up the wrong tree. Shari's heart belongs to another man."

"Who is he?" he demanded, looking around, agitated. "I'll punch his lights out. I'll rip his lungs out. I'll —"

"Forget it, Ramon. It's nobody you know. He lives in another town. To tell you the truth, she seems like an airhead, anyway."

"Bummer." Ramon collected up his books, glancing at Shari's table. "Well, if you tune in on any other girls who like me, let me know, will ya, Jake?"

"Sure thing, Ramon."

One day before practice, Coach Rosario pulled me aside. He had a rolled up newspaper in his hand.

"Jake, I want to ask you a question," the coach said, guiding me over to the bleachers.

He opened up the newspaper to the business section and laid it out before me.

"Do you see anything here, Jake?" he asked. "Anything at all?"

"Sure, Coach, that's the stock market pages."

"I know *that*, Jake. But does it make anything pop into your head? Do you see any specific stocks going way up tomorrow? Or way down? Any movement at all?"

I glanced up at Coach Rosario. He looked kind of sheepish.

"I was just thinking," he said. "Maybe I — I mean *you* and I — could make a little money with your special, uh, talent."

I looked at the paper and focused all my energy on it. Nothing happened. "Sorry, Coach," I said, shaking my head. "I'm not picking anything up."

He turned to the sports section and opened the paper up to the page on horse racing.

"Anything here?" he asked, glancing at his watch. "Does anything about the fifth race at

50

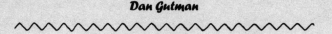
Belmont jump out at you? Of course, I would give you half of anything we won."

I looked down at the paper and focused on it full blast.

"Sorry, Coach, I don't see anything. I guess I only have the power to read minds. I can't predict what will happen tomorrow."

"Too bad," Coach Rosario muttered as he shuffled away and slapped out a fungo.

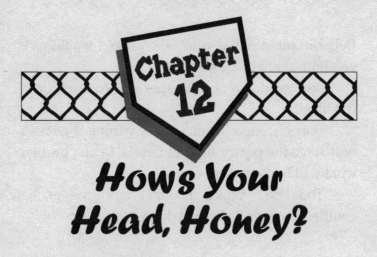

How's Your Head, Honey?

The season ended, and we blew the doors off the rest of the teams in the National League. I chipped in with a .422 average, seven homers, and countless stolen signals that led to victories for our team. Coach Rosario awarded me the team's Most Valuable Player award.

In the American League, Whip led his team to the pennant, which meant that the Martinizers and the Hornets would meet in a one-game, do-or-die, battle-to-the-death championship. The Hornets would be very tough to beat, even if I could steal their signs.

*   *   *   *

We were sitting around the dinner table a week before the big game when the phone rang. I ran into the den and picked it up.

"Jake?" a man's voice said.

"Yes?"

"This is Dr. Kielbasa."

"Oh, hi. How ya doin'?"

"Good. Jake, do you remember I told you I was thinking of shooting an MRI of your brain?"

"Yes."

"Well, the hospital was finally able to squeeze you into the schedule. Tell your mom or dad to bring you over at eleven o'clock on Saturday morning, okay? I won't be there, but the technicians will take good care of you."

"But I have a game on Saturday morning. It's the World Series."

"I'm sorry, Jake, that's the only time they can take you."

There was no *way* I was going to miss the game. It was useless to argue with him, so I told the doctor okay and hung up the phone. I just won't show up for the appointment, I decided. What could they do, kidnap me? Throw me in jail?

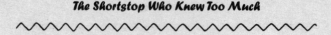

"Who was that, sweetie?" Mom asked when I came back to the table.

"Uh, just somebody who wanted you to switch long-distance companies," I lied. "I told 'em to buzz off."

I had to lie. If my folks knew I was scheduled for an MRI at the same time as the game, they might do something crazy like force me to skip the game.

In the days leading up to the big game my parents — especially Mom — got all worked up and nervous. "How's your head, honey?" she kept asking me. "Are you sure you're going to be able to play?"

It didn't take a mind reader to see what was bothering Mom. She knew I'd be facing Whip for the first time since he nailed me with that pitch. She was afraid I might get hit in the head again. My dad was concerned that I'd be so afraid of Whip's fastball, I'd make a fool of myself bailing out of the batter's box. I had the feeling that they didn't want me to play.

"I'm playing," I told them both firmly. "That's final."

*   *   *   *

I laid my uniform out carefully on Friday night before the game. It was crisp. It smelled good. Those martinizers really know their martinizing. I ran my hand across the big M on the chest. With my pants, jersey, socks, and cap laid out on the floor, it looked like the invisible man was lying there.

I crawled into bed (with my glove, as always) but had a hard time getting to sleep. Every time I zonked out, I would start dreaming about Whip's fastball. It came at me overhand. It came at me sidearm. It came at me underhand. No matter which way it came at me, it always ended up the same way — smashing against my head. That's when I'd wake up.

I had to admit it at least to myself — I was scared.

I don't know if I ever fell completely asleep. Dad woke up when he heard me brushing my teeth in the morning.

"Want a lift to the game, Jake?" he asked, padding around in his pajamas.

"No thanks," I told him. "I feel like biking it, Dad."

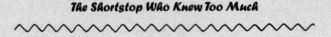

"Okay, Mom and I will meet you there." Dad looked me in the eye and asked, "Are you gonna be okay, Jake? You don't have to play, you know."

I gave him the thumbs-up sign and punched him in the stomach lightly. Dad and I used to hug and kiss a lot when I was little, but now I think we both feel more comfortable wrestling and hitting each other and stuff. He socked me in the shoulder and said, "Go get 'em, Jake."

I shoveled down some Crispix before putting on my uniform and heading out for the biggest game of my life.

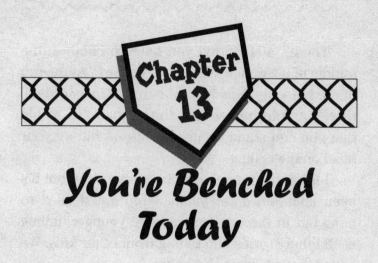

Chapter 13

You're Benched Today

Kroeger Field, where we play most of our games, is about a mile away. To get there by bike, I go through Ivy Hill Park. It's sort of a junky old park. Half the time the swings are wrapped around their poles. The seesaws were stolen years ago. Not many kids go to Ivy Hill anymore, but when Whip and I were younger it was our second home.

I tossed my glove in my backpack and wheeled out of the garage.

Almost as soon as I turned the corner, I felt a funny, unsettling feeling, like something was wrong but I couldn't put my finger on it. I kept looking around, but didn't see anything. The feeling grew stronger the closer I got to Kroeger Field.

There's a steep hill you have to climb in the middle of a wooded section of the park. At the top of the hill, only a quarter mile from Kroeger Field, there's an old tunnel next to the road. It's so big that you can stand up inside without hitting your head on the ceiling.

I think the tunnel used to carry water, but it's been abandoned for years. Whip and I used to hang out in there when we were younger, telling each other stories and hiding from other kids. We called it our "secret clubhouse."

I clicked my bike into tenth gear and pedaled furiously so I could build up enough momentum to make it up the hill. Nobody wants to be seen pushing his bike up the hill.

I was moving pretty fast, but by the time I had reached the top of the hill, the bike had slowed down so much it was barely moving.

Suddenly, out of the corner of my eye, I saw two figures jump out of the tunnel and run toward me.

I didn't get a look at their faces. One of them slapped his hand over my mouth and grabbed me from behind. The other one put a blindfold over

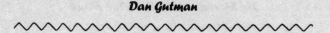

my eyes. They wrestled me off my bike and hustled me into the tunnel.

"Leave me alone!" I tried to shout as they tied me up. "I gotta get to a game!"

"The game'll go on just fine without you, Kreskin," one of the guys said, laughing. "You're benched today."

I knew Kreskin was the name of a celebrity who was famous for being able to read minds. These guys must know about my ESP.

They tied my feet together and my hands behind my back. I couldn't see because of the blindfold, and they put a gag in my mouth to prevent me from shouting. They were being careful not to hurt me. It seemed like they only wanted to keep me there for awhile.

When they were finished tying me up, one of them held a rag against my nose. It had a strong odor, a smell I had never smelled before.

"Who *are* you?" I mumbled through the gag.

"I thought he could read minds," one of them said as he threw a heavy blanket over me. "He should be able to figure out who we are."

I tried to focus my attention on them, but the

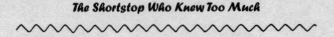

smell from the rag was making me feel light-headed. I couldn't tune into their thoughts, and I didn't recognize their voices.

"So long, Houdini!" one of them called as they dashed out the tunnel.

"Too bad you're gonna miss your game!" the other one said, laughing.

That was the last thing I heard before I fell asleep.

Delay of Game

I don't know how much time passed before I came to. It could have been a few minutes, or it could have been a few hours. As I lay there, trapped, I tried to figure out who would hate me enough to have me kidnapped and thrown in a tunnel.

Whip! Of course! He was steamed because I wouldn't talk to him. He knows this tunnel, too.

Nah! That's not Whip's style. He'd rather beat me on the field than do something cowardly like this.

Molly! It must have been Molly! She was still mad about losing the Griffey card, and she didn't like it when I used my ESP to impress the teachers at school.

Nah! Molly is on my team and she really wants to win that trip to Cooperstown. She might not like me, but she would want me in the game. Kids don't kidnap anyway. It had to be a grown-up. But who?

I heard some cars going by, but my muffled yells barely made it past the blanket surrounding me. I tried to get my hands free, but they were tied expertly.

Whoever did this was pretty smart, it occurred to me. They must have hired people I didn't know to kidnap me, so that if I *did* read their minds, I wouldn't know who was behind it. Clever. Somebody wanted to keep me out of the game pretty badly.

Maybe it was the coach of the Hornets, I thought. He knew that if he could get me out of the game, his team would have a big advantage. Not very sportsmanlike, but grown-ups can be that way sometimes.

There was nothing I could do except lie back and hope somebody stumbled upon me.

I had plenty to think about, and plenty of time to think. I used the time to make my mind up about one thing — I decided that I was going to give up mind reading. It was a pretty cool gift to have, but it was just getting me into trouble. And like Molly said, using ESP was sort of like cheating your way through life. I wanted to make it on my own.

At least a half an hour passed since I had woken up. The game had certainly started. It might even be *over*. I was sure my parents were out looking for me, but they couldn't stop the game. There's a league rule that says if a player is more than ten minutes late, the team has to start another player in the first player's place.

Suddenly I heard the sound of sneakers coming from the roadway. I tried to yell. The sneakers stopped right outside the tunnel and rustled the leaves inside.

"Jake?" yelled a voice.

Somebody ripped the blanket away and untied the blindfold.

"Whip!" I shouted through the gag. "I'm so happy to see you!"

"If you're still mad at me," he said, "I could just leave you here, man."

"Untie my hands so I can punch you in the nose!" I shouted. "How'd you find me?"

"I looked everywhere else, man! This was the last place I could think of. The police are looking

63

all over for you! It's like a manhunt! Your parents are going bananas! They've probably got your picture on milk cartons already!"

"Who won the game?" I asked.

"It hasn't begun, Jake! You don't think they'd start without the stars of each team, do you?"

"Why'd you come looking for me, Whip? You could have done nothing and breezed through the game."

"Because you're my best friend, man," he said.

I looked him in the eye. There was no need to read his mind. He was telling the truth.

We found my bike hidden in the bushes near the tunnel. Whip and I walked the short distance to Kroeger Field together, our arms around one another.

The tiny bleachers were filled with people, and more were sitting on lawn chairs and spread out on blankets on the grass. I'd never seen so many spectators at one of our games before.

As Whip and I approached the field, a buzz spread through the stands, and then cheers. The crowd parted to let us through like we were Mark McGwire and Randy Johnson.

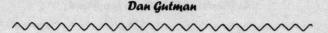

"Hey," Whip whispered, "check out who's sitting at the end of the second row, first base side."

I peered over there and scanned the row until I saw a familiar face.

It was Rosalie Minder, the queen of the Somerville Fall Festival parade! She was the girl Whip and I had been fighting about before he beaned me.

"She's mine," Whip said.

"Mine," I insisted.

"Mine. I called first."

"Mine-mine-mine-mine," I replied quickly. "Foursies overrules first calls."

"Does not."

"Does too."

Whip and I burst out laughing.

My parents rushed over and Mom threw her arms around me. "Jake, I was so worried! Where were you?"

"I was tied up," I said, throwing Whip a wink. "Everything's okay now."

When I got to our bench everybody gathered around me like I was a conquering hero. Molly was the first to get to me.

"Jake, whatever happened to you, I want you

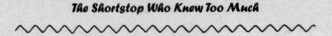

to know I had nothing to do with it. If you don't believe me, read my mind."

"No sweat, Molly," I said, "Let's go win this thing."

"Coaches," bellowed the ump, looking at his watch. "Do you have all your players *now*?"

Both coaches shouted that they did.

"Then let's play some ball!"

Chapter 15

The First Inning

The Hornets are sponsored by Hornan Hardware. The owner, Joe Hornan, likes to dream up hardware-related cheers for the team. Half the crowd began chanting . . .

Chop 'em! Saw 'em!
Nail 'em! Plane 'em!
Before we're done,
We'll sand 'em and stain 'em!

I pulled Coach Rosario aside as he was rewriting his lineup card.

"Coach, I need to talk to you about something."

"Sure, Jake. Everything okay? How's the brain? All systems go?"

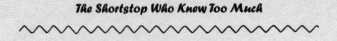

"Yeah, I'm fine, Coach. But I've decided to play the game straight. No mind reading."

Coach Rosario's eyes opened wide. "Wait a minute," he said, hitting his head with the palm of his hand. "I must have something stuck in my ears. I thought I just heard you say you weren't going to use your ESP."

"I'm not, Coach. I've been thinking about it, and I decided that it's not fair to read minds and steal signs to win. It feels like cheating. I want to see if we can beat these guys fair and square. Our best against their best. No tricks."

The coach turned to me and put an arm on my shoulder. "Jake," he said slowly, "do you think Wayne Gretzky plays hockey in his old, worn-out, dull skates?"

"No . . ."

"Of course, he doesn't. He wears the sharpest, newest, best skates money can buy."

"I know, Coach . . ."

"Gretzky is the best in the world. Do you think he skates a little slower so the other team can catch up with him?"

"Of course not, Coach . . ."

"He skates as fast as he can, right? And do you think Shaquille O'Neal misses shots on purpose once in a while so he won't make the other basketball players feel bad that they're not as good as he is?"

"No, but, Coach, this is diff —"

"And when Tony Gwynn comes to the plate, do you think he ever says, 'I'm better than everybody else here. So today I'm going to bat with one eye closed'?"

"No."

"Then why do you want to handicap yourself? You've got a one-in-a-million talent, Jake! *Use* it! An athlete has to use every tool he has. Do you think Whip Witherspoon is gonna ease up on us today because he's such a good pitcher? You know that if the Hornets had a guy who could read minds they'd steal all *our* signs."

"Then *they'd* be cheating, Coach!" I had made up my mind. "If I read their minds and we win this game, I would feel like we never really won the championship."

Coach Rosario didn't like it, but he seemed to understand what I was trying to say. "Okay, Jake,"

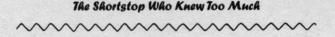

he sighed. "I would never force you to do what you don't want to do. But will you do me one favor? Don't tell the team that you're not going to use ESP. It gives 'em confidence knowing you've got everything figured out."

"Okay, Coach," I said. "I won't."

Coach Rosario got up and started walking toward the umpire to discuss the ground rules, then stopped and turned to me. "Jake," he said, pointing his finger at me, "I still expect you to win this game for us."

Before Whip and I arrived on the field, the two coaches had flipped a coin and determined that the Martinizers would be the home team. So we would take the field first, and we would get last licks.

Nail 'em! Glue 'em!
Stick duct tape to 'em!
If that doesn't work,
We'll put nuts and bolts through 'em!

The crowd settled into their seats. Jack Atkinson, the mayor of Somerville, walked out to home plate to address the crowd.

"Ladies and gentlemen," he boomed into the microphone. "Welcome to the Junior World Series of Somerville! I can't tell you how proud I am of all these young men and women. I'm sure you are just as proud of them. Whichever team wins today, you have all done a terrific job this season. Let's give the players a round of applause."

Applause applause applause.

"The winning team, as you know, will get a free trip to the Baseball Hall of Fame in Cooperstown, New York, thanks to the good folks at the Allied National Bank. So now we know what they're doing with all our money, right?"

The grown-ups laughed.

"We have another prize, too," Mayor Atkinson added. "The Most Valuable Player of today's game will receive a kiss from either the king or queen of the Somerville Fall Festival parade, Phil Veloric or Rosalie Minder, take your pick!"

The crowd hooted and whistled. Some of the kids on our bench yelled, "Yuck, disgusting!" Whip and I looked at each other from across the field. I pointed to my chest and mouthed the words, "She's mine." Whip did the same thing.

When the Martinizers trotted out on the field,

a roar went up from the crowd. It was only the Junior World Series of Somerville, New Jersey, but it felt like the *real* World Series.

It felt great to be out there. I smoothed the dirt around the shortstop position with a sweep of my foot. Ramon Martinez tossed me a few sharp grounders. I scooped them cleanly and rifled the ball back to him at first base. I was ready. The ump pulled a fresh, white baseball from his bag and tossed it to our pitcher, Joey Risko.

The leadoff batter for the Hornets was the nerdy son of Dr. Kielbasa. He was real skinny and the bridge of his glasses was taped together.

Joey must have been a little nervous because he walked the Kielbasa kid on four pitches. Joey wasn't way off the plate, but just enough so the ump wouldn't give him a strike call. The Kielbasa kid looked like he wasn't going to swing, no matter what. Maybe he was nervous, too.

I trotted out to the mound. "Not to worry," I said, putting my arm around Joey. "I looked into my crystal ball, and it said you whiff the next guy."

Joey grinned. He wasn't sure if I was kidding or not. I was, but I wasn't about to tell *him* that. In any case, Joey pumped in strike one right over the plate. The batter was taking all the way.

If I had been using my ESP, I would focus in on the runner at first and the opposing coach to see if they were planning a steal. But because I had decided not to use ESP, I had to rely on my wits.

I looked at the Kielbasa kid at first base. He was probably anxious to impress his dad in the stands. A big threat to steal.

I looked at the Hornets' coach, and he was staring at me with a quizzical expression on his face. He was trying to figure me out. I stared back at him with a knowing smile. Then I put two fingers behind my head and wiggled them around like they were antennae. Just for good measure, I stuck my tongue out at him.

The coach turned away disgustedly. He didn't flash any signs to the Kielbasa kid.

Joey pumped the next pitch over the plate. The hitter swung and missed. The Kielbasa kid didn't take a step off first base.

The Hornets' coach must be afraid to take any chances on me. It occurred to me that having people *believe* I have ESP is just about as good as *having* ESP. I decided it's all right to play with *their* minds, even if it's not all right to play with my own.

Joey tossed in strike three, called. One out.

The hitter dragged his bat to the bench. The Kielbasa kid kicked the first base bag in frustration. He wanted to run. Joe sneaked a peek at me and flashed a smile. I tapped my forehead with my index finger and yelled loud enough for everybody to hear, "It's all up here, Joey baby!"

The next batter tapped an easy grounder my way on the first pitch. I smothered it on two hops and shoveled it to Molly. She stepped on second base and winged the ball to Ramon at first. Double play! Just like in practice. We were out of the inning, and we high-fived our way to the bench.

Whip looked impressive taking his warm-ups. The rest of us looked like a bunch of kids playing ball, but Whip looked like a *ballplayer*. It was something in the way he carried himself. He had that casual confidence major leaguers have. The great ones are born with it, I suppose.

Before Ramon Martinez went to the plate to lead off for the Martinizers, Coach Rosario gathered us around him.

"Listen up, everybody," he said. "Whip Wither-spoon throws hard, we all know that." A few heads turned to glance at me. "I don't want to see any of you swinging for the fences to impress your moms and dads out there. That will only produce a lot of strikeouts, believe me. Just try and meet the ball. Get the bat on it. The harder the pitch, the harder it comes back at them. Okay, Ramon, go get 'em!"

We put our hands together and let out a loud collective *whoop*.

Whip took his last warm-up pitch and Ramon dug in at the plate. Whip's first pitch exploded in the catcher's mitt with a *pop* that echoed across the field. Strike one.

Ramon was trying to act cool about it, but anybody could see he was shaking in his spikes. He's a pretty good hitter. But when you're used to kids throwing 40 or 50 miles per hour, it's hard to adjust to 60 or 70 miles per hour. And it's scary.

"Be aggressive, Ramon," I shouted helpfully. But I could see that as Whip went into his windup, Ramon was already moving his back foot away from the plate. Foot in the bucket, they call it. It's

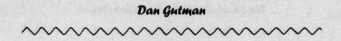

a sure sign of fear. Strike two popped into the catcher's mitt.

Ramon shook his head as he stepped out of the batter's box and rubbed the palms of his hands on his pants.

Whip threw the next pitch way outside, trying to get Ramon to fish for strike three. Ramon didn't bite. The count was one and two. Then Whip tried to nip the outside corner, and Ramon kept the bat on his shoulder. That put the count at two balls and two strikes.

Whip must have decided to stop fooling around. He came at Ramon with smoke, right over the plate. Ramon took a big cut at it, but he was late.

"Steeeeeeerike three!" yelled the ump. The Hornets whooped it up. Ramon walked back to our bench glumly.

Molly was up next, and she looked even worse than Ramon. Whip blew her away with three fastballs.

"Where was that last pitch?" asked Coach Rosario as Molly came back to the bench.

"How should I know?" she replied, "I didn't even see it."

We all laughed, but it was nervous laughter. Nobody wanted to be in the batter's box when Whip Witherspoon was having a good day.

From the on-deck circle, I could tell Whip had great stuff. Maybe his best ever. Whip and I had practically been born with bats and balls in our hands. I had hit against him hundreds of times at his house, at my house, at the playground. But I had never seen him throw so hard or with more confidence.

A hush fell over the crowd as I stepped up to the plate with two outs. Everyone knew this was the first meeting between Whip and me since he nearly decapitated me in that warm-up game before the season started. Many people knew about the bad blood between us. A few suspected I had ESP. Only Coach Rosario and I knew I wasn't using it.

Whip nodded to me and I nodded back. We were friends again. But during the time that he was on the mound and I was in the batter's box, we would always be enemies.

I dug my left foot into the chalk line at the back of the box. With a pitcher as fast as Whip, you want to be as far back as possible so you can have

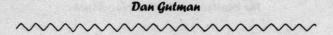

more time to look over each pitch. I was determined to stay in there and get my three licks no matter how much heat Whip threw at me.

I tried to put the beaning out of my mind. It was tough, though. The nightmares of Whip nailing me were fresh in my mind. I tightened my grip on the bat and concentrated on Whip's left hand.

"Go for it, Jake!" somebody on our bench shouted.

"You can do it!" yelled Coach Rosario.

"I CLEAN! YOU CLEAN! THE BEST CLEAN IS DRY CLEAN!" chanted the Martinizers from the bench. (The Hornets clearly had it all over us when it came to chanting. There's just not a whole lot you can say about dry cleaning).

"Strike him out, Whip!" shouted a voice from the Hornet side.

Whip's first pitch to me sailed far outside, skidding past the catcher and all the way to the backstop. Both of us laughed. Whip was just as scared of hitting me again as I was that he was going to hit me. Ball one.

The next pitch was closer to the outside corner and I took a swipe at it. The ball ticked off the end of my bat and skittered down the right field line. I asked the ump for time and stepped out of the box. One ball and one strike.

"He's hittable," I told my teammates.

I fouled off the next pitch, too, beating the ball into the dirt. Whip had me at a ball and two strikes.

The wheels in my head were turning. He might try to waste a pitch off the outside corner. Then again, he might come right after me. Whip, I remembered, loves to strike out the side. I choked up on the bat an inch or two to protect the plate.

Whip reared back, kicked up his leg and threw. The pitch looked fat and I started my swing. The ball was about halfway to the plate when I realized I was swinging early. He had fooled me with a slow change-up.

I tried to slow the swing down and just foul the ball off, but my timing was messed up. The ball plopped softly into the catcher's mitt and I swung like a kid in his first T-ball game.

Strike three. Side retired. No score at the end of the first inning.

"You expect to get anybody out throwing that junk?" I yelled at Whip as he strolled off the mound.

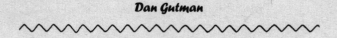
Whip laughed. "Got *you* out," he said.

As I grabbed my glove and went back out to the shortstop position, I thought how the game might have been different if I was using my ESP. I would have known Whip was going to throw his change-up. I might have slammed it over the wall. But he struck me out fair and square.

The Middle Innings

In the second inning, Joey retired the Hornets 1, 2, 3, and Whip struck out the side again. The game was shaping up to be a pitchers' duel.

Joey was pitching a gutsy game, probably the best of his life. He didn't have Whip's speed, but Joey is a competitor. He gave the Hornets a few hits, but then he would bear down on the next batter and get him out.

Our defense was airtight. We were making all the routine plays, and when we needed a great play one of us would come through with it. That Kielbasa kid hit a pop fly to short right field that was too deep for Molly at second and too shallow

for our right fielder. Molly ran out full speed with her back to the plate and snared the ball just before it hit the ground. It was one for the highlights video, for sure.

But all the defense in the world won't do you any good if you can't score a run. Whip was striking out almost all of us, and the others hit easy dribblers to the infield. I'd never seen him so fast. He could have had his outfielders sit on the bench. None of us could get the ball out there. The score was 0–0.

Around the fourth inning, a buzz started going around that Whip was working on a no-hitter. He'd never pitched a "no-no" before. In fact, in the history of the Somerville Little League, there had never been a no-hitter. Whip, I knew, would die to throw a no-no in a game this important.

In our league, the pitchers usually don't go more than three or four innings. But there was no tomorrow. This would be the last game of the season. Joey and Whip both went out to pitch the fifth inning. I had a feeling that whichever pitcher faltered would be the loser.

They were both getting tired. Joey's pitches

looked like they were in super slo-mo, and it was just dumb luck that the Hornets didn't score off him in the fifth inning.

Whip was losing velocity, too. Bubba Bradley hit a screamer off him, but their left fielder caught it with his back against the fence. Whip still had his no-hitter at the end of five innings, and the score was still tied at nothing.

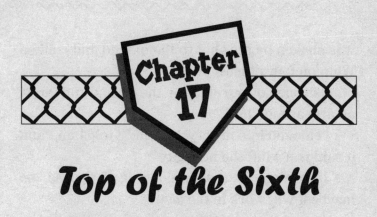

Chapter 17

Top of the Sixth

And then came the sixth inning. The final inning. Joey looked like he was ready to collapse as he took the mound. Coach Rosario had tried to bring in another pitcher, but Joey talked him out of it.

"No way," he said. "I started this thing, and I'm gonna finish it."

The first Hornet batter hit a bullet — an absolute bullet — right back to the mound. Joey put his glove up in self-defense. The ball ricocheted off the glove and rolled toward first. Ramon dashed over from his first base position, snatched the ball up, and stepped on the bag just before the runner. Miracle play. One out.

Whip was up next for the Hornets. He's a decent hitter, but he's tall and lanky so his strike zone is pretty big. Even so, Joey couldn't find it. He

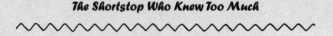

was shaken by the shot to the mound and walked Whip on four pitches.

I strolled over to Joey on the mound and threw an arm around him.

"I looked into my crystal ball," I told him, "and it said you whiff the next guy."

It worked in the first inning, I figured, so maybe it will work in the last.

Joey got two quick strikes on the batter and he sneaked me a wicked smile. His confidence was high. Whip took a lead from first base. He could steal a base if he had to, and the Hornets could sure use a stolen base here.

I glanced at the coach of the Hornets, and he was staring back at me. The Hornets hadn't tried to steal a base all game. They figured that if they tried, I would see it a mile away and call for a pitchout.

Whip's coach flashed him a series of signs. I had no idea what they meant, but I had a feeling. In the last inning of a scoreless game, the Hornets needed to get a run *now*. Even if I *was* reading their signs, it might be worth the risk to have Whip try and steal.

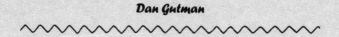

I signaled our catcher Bubba Bradley for a pitchout on the next pitch. Whip took his lead. Joey took his windup.

Whip was running! Bubba leaped out from behind the plate. The batter took a wild swing and missed the ball by a mile. Strike three. I scooted over to the second base bag. Bubba pumped the ball to me.

Whip hit the dirt headfirst. Bubba's throw was right there. I snatched it out of the air and brought my glove down in front of the bag. Whip's hands slid right into my glove. It was a thing of beauty.

"Yer ouuuuuut!" screamed the ump. Double play. Side retired. Whip lay in the dirt at second base. He was clearly exhausted. I reached out a hand to help him up, and he grabbed it.

"This is some kind of game, isn't it?" I said.

"Some kind of game," agreed Whip.

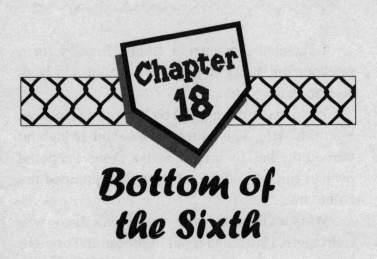

Bottom of
the Sixth

So this was it. The bottom of the sixth. Still no
score. We're up for our last licks. If we can put a
run across the plate here, the game is over. Whip is
still on the mound.

Bubba Bradley, batting seventh for us, led off.
Whip got two strikes on him, and then Bubba
tapped a weak roller back to Whip. He threw to
first and Bubba was out of there. One out.

Our left fielder, Phil Denlinger, was up next.
Whip fanned him, his twelfth strikeout of the
game. Two outs. It wasn't looking good for the
Martinizers.

Our number nine hitter was Joey. He had

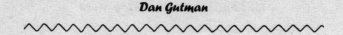

pitched a great game, and received a big ovation when he stepped up to the plate.

On Whip's first pitch, Joey hit a grounder to third. It wasn't hit hard, but the third baseman bobbled the ball and made a wild throw to first. Joey went to second on the overthrow.

The umpire ruled it an error. Whip still had his no-hitter, but we had a runner in scoring position. A single would win the game.

The top of the order — Ramon Martinez — was coming up. Whip had been striking Ramon out all day, but not this time. Whip looked like he was rattled by the error. He walked Ramon. That put runners on first and second with two outs.

Molly Carver was up, and I went out to the on-deck circle.

"He's tired now," she told me. "I'm takin' him downtown."

"Just get your bat on the ball," I urged her. "A single wins the game and you're the hero."

Whip got two balls and two strikes on Molly. She took a cut at the next pitch and slapped a grounder to short.

The shortstop fielded the ball cleanly. He

could have made the easy play to first for the third out to end the inning. Instead, he decided to go for the force play at third base. As the ball arrived, Joey barreled into third in a cloud of dust.

The third baseman dropped the ball.

"Saaaafe!" boomed the umpire.

Safe all around. Now we had the bases loaded — Joey on third, Ramon on second, and Molly on first. And I'm up.

Gulp.

I thought of all the things that could happen for us to win this game. I could get a hit, of course. Whip could walk me and force in the winning run. Somebody could make an error. Whip could wild pitch the run home. Or there could be a passed ball.

Lots of ways to win. And Whip is tired. We had a lot going for us.

Coach Rosario came over to me. "Jake," he said, putting an arm on my shoulder, "it's not too late to change your mind. Use your ESP, son! Find out what he's gonna throw you and then whale it."

"No," I replied. "I'm gonna do it my way, Coach."

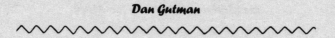

"Okay, Jake. You're the boss. Give it your best shot."

This at-bat is going to be one of those memories I'll have for the rest of my life, I thought as I stepped up to the plate.

Whip and I looked at one another and nodded slightly. It was all business now. No smiles. The beaning was gone from our minds. We were both concentrating on right now.

The crowd was silent. They even stopped selling ice cream in the snack bar.

Whip burned in strike one almost before I had the chance to dig into the batter's box. The next pitch was high so I let it go by. One ball, one strike.

Whip's next pitch was outside, but the umpire called it a strike anyway. I didn't complain. Umpires make mistakes, and they're under a lot of pressure, too. Meanwhile, the count was one ball and two strikes. I had to protect the plate.

Whip put a little extra on the next pitch, but he overthrew it and it sailed high. The catcher had to reach up at the last instant to snare the ball. On the next pitch, Whip tried to adjust and the ball went in the dirt. Again the catcher made a good play to stop it.

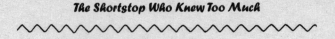

It was a full count. Bottom of the sixth. No score. Bases loaded. Two outs.

I stepped out of the box and Whip stepped off the mound. The tension was too much for either of us.

All day long I had resisted the temptation to use my ESP. It would be so simple now, I thought to myself. Just read Whip's mind, find out what the next pitch will be, and smash it. If there was ever a time to use my secret weapon, this was it.

One side of my head was telling me: "No! Don't! You've come so far this way! Don't ruin it now!"

The other side was telling me: "Go for it! Just this one time. Nobody will ever know. You'll be the hero!"

I would like to tell you that I decided not to use my ESP. I would like to tell you that, but I can't. I wanted to do the right thing, but I guess I wanted to win the game even more. I stepped back in the box and focused my attention on Whip like a laser beam.

"Fastball, low and outside," he was thinking.

Okay, here it comes, I thought to myself. I'm ready for it.

For a millisecond or two, I thought about moving my head backward so the ball would *whoosh* by in front of me. For another millisecond, I thought about moving my head forward so the ball would zip behind me.

But once again, I ran out of milliseconds and simply stood there. "Duck!" was the last word I heard before the baseball exploded against my head.

As I crumpled to the ground, I heard somebody yelling that we won the game 1–0. By hitting me with the bases loaded, Whip had forced in the winning run. But at the moment I wasn't thinking about winning or losing.

When I opened my eyes a few seconds later, Dr. Kielbasa was leaning over me and holding my head. "You're gonna be okay, Jake," he said. "But next time, do what your doctor tells you to do. If

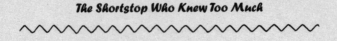

you had gone for the MRI this wouldn't have happened."

I focused my attention on Dr. Kielbasa and couldn't help but read his mind: **"How did he *get* here? I told them to keep him away from the game. I can't believe this happened! It just goes to show that if you want a job done right, do it yourself."**

I sat bolt upright and pointed at Dr. Kielbasa. "So it was *you*! You had me kidnapped! You knew I could read minds and you wanted to keep me out of the game so your son's team would win! That's why you scheduled the MRI at the same time as the game! You oughta be ashamed of yourself!"

"He's delirious," Dr. Kielbasa explained to everybody gathered around me. "He's ranting. Somebody call an ambulance."

I don't know what happened next, because everything went black.

When I woke up, I was on a stretcher, and an ambulance was right out on the field next to me. One of the guys on the ambulance squad was taking my pulse. "You'll be okay," he said.

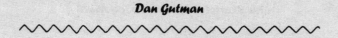

I figured I'd read his mind to see if he was telling the truth. I looked at him and concentrated, but I didn't hear anything. "This guy must be really stupid," I said to myself. "He doesn't have a thought in his head."

Wait a minute. That wasn't it. It wasn't that the guy was stupid. I just couldn't read his mind.

My ESP was no longer working!

The first bonk on the head gave me ESP and the second bonk must have caused it to fade away. Now the power was completely gone.

So was Dr. Kielbasa. He must have figured I was going to expose him, so he hightailed it out of there. My parents and Mayor Atkinson were staring down at me. I tried to figure out what they were thinking, but I was picking up nothing.

"How do you feel son?" the mayor asked.

"Okay," I said, feeling my head all over for bumps. "Actually, I feel pretty good."

"Good enough to accept the Most Valuable Player award?"

With that, he led Rosalie Minder over to me. She gave me a plaque and planted a kiss on my lips.

"Congratulations," she said. "You deserve *two* kisses after *this* game."

I looked around to find Whip. I wanted to make sure he saw Rosalie kissing me. I didn't have to look far. Whip ran over, bawling like a baby.

"I'm sorry, Jake!" he blubbered. "I didn't mean it, man! The pitch got away from me. It was an accident! I swear it's true!"

"I know, Whip," I said. "I know."

It didn't take a mind reader to know Whip was telling the truth.

Note to the reader

ESP or extrasensory perception, is a "sixth sense" that many people claim to have. Some have said they can read minds. Others say they can hear voices of the dead, predict events that haven't taken place yet, or somehow know who committed crimes that baffle the police.

The existence of ESP has never been proven scientifically in a laboratory setting, and virtually all scientists believe it does not exist.

About the Author

Dan Gutman has always loved baseball, but when he was growing up he wasn't a very good player. "I was afraid of getting hit with the ball," he says. But that didn't stop him from enjoying the game and learning everything he could about it.

In the last few years, Dan has written seven factual books about baseball, including *Baseball's Greatest Games* and *Baseball's Biggest Bloopers*, and one fictional story, *They Came From Center-field*, published in 1995. He had so much fun writing the story that he wanted to do more, so he came up with the idea for this series. The first four *Tales from the Sandlot* will be published this year.

In between sports stories, Dan wrote *The Kid Who Ran for President*, a funny story about a twelve-year-old who runs for president of the United States. It was published in 1996.

When he's not writing, Dan can often be found visiting classrooms, where he talks to students about baseball and writing books. He lives in Haddonfield, New Jersey, with his wife and two young children.